# New Normal

# New Normal

Amber Cloves

LIFE RATTLE PRESS

New Normal

Published by Life Rattle Press, Toronto, Canada

Life Rattle New Writers Series



ISBN: 978-1-987936-31-5

Cover design by Amber Cloves
Copy edited by Lyndsay Sinko

*This is for my family.*

1 in 5 Canadians will personally experience a mental illness in their lifetime.

-Canadian Mental Health Association, (2016)

# Table of Contents

# Almond Eyes
*October 2nd, 2011*

# *Rose*

I sit in a plastic maroon chair, my snow boots swinging back and forth from beneath my green wooden desk. My fingers absentmindedly trace the carved-in doodles that riddle the wood. My eyes lock onto the analog clock. 3:20. Five more minutes until freedom.

"Before class ends, don't forget to take home your class selection signup sheets for next year," announces Mr. Mcneill, my grade eleven homeroom teacher. "I need this back. Seriously. Or you're stuck with me again. And don't forget the report cards, I need those parental signatures," he pauses.

"*Not* friends' signatures." He adds as he scans the room, making obvious eye contact with Jenna, Laurie and Michael.

Mr. McNeill runs his hands through his hair and gives us a crooked smile. I join in as the class utters a collective groan.

"Okay, everyone. Pack up and line up by the door, I can tell everyone's done for the day. You are released."

The class scrambles to their feet and the room fills with the buzz of animated talking, backpacks zipping and chairs being pulled from their desks. Mr. McNeill hands me a sign-up sheet and I bolt out the classroom, and head for my locker.

⌘

Okay, so we've covered Math, English, Yearbook, Dance, Communication Technology, what about French?" My mother asks. I watch as she balances her Samsung smartphone against her right ear as she takes calls from work, Durham District School Board.

We sit at the kitchen table, reviewing next year's course selection. The cool surface of the table makes goosebumps ripple up my arms and I shift in my seat, tapping my pen on the side of my chair. The open report card rests beside us. With an eighty-two average, there's nothing to hide.

Mum scans though the signup sheet with her alert hazel eyes. Her dark blonde and brown hair tucks neatly behind her left ear. Mum is a supply teacher, meaning her schedule is always changing. I watch as she doodles flowers onto the crumpled and filled out calendar beside her.

"Oh no, that was my lowest grade all year." I can hear the whine in my voice and cringe.

"But you did great last year, Oh wait, sorry Rose-"

Her phone connects.

"Thursday teaching gym at Rosebank? Sure, I'll take it. Thanks Sue. Okay, bye now." She scribbles the date onto her calendar, puts the cell on the table, and stares at me.

"Okay. What's wrong with French?" She looks at me with a dark eyebrow arched.

"I understood last year's teacher better. She doesn't teach grade eleven french though."

"I can help you with it next year. I'm already tutoring the Johnson kids with their french, so we can do the same thing," my mother explains.

I frown. "Yeah? Are you sure...it was hard for me. I don't learn from Madame Mraz, and she's the one who teaches it, remember? I had to switch out in grade nine."

"We can do it together, don't worry. Besides, a smart kid like you will have no trouble." She smiles, proud, and nods to the open report card.

My lips scrunch together. Mum gives me a warm smile. It's settled. French for me.

"...okay then," I mutter while circling the French academic option on the signup sheet with red ink.

⌘

All around me is the scratchy, faint sound of pencils on paper. Everyone in class furiously scribbles at their French unit tests. Everyone, except me.

I sit there as my eyes turn blurry, trying to blink back tears. My chest is tight and my head throbs at the verbs I'm supposed to conjugate in front of me. Time passes, but my concentration is shot.

My fists clench around my pencil so hard, my pale knuckles turn white. Instead of deciphering the sentences in front of me, my eyes find the clock. 2:00.

Half an hour and I'm outta here.

I'm pulled out of my thoughts as our teacher, Madame Mraz, brings her small, dainty hands to her cool, collected face.

"Ahem." She clears her voice, her bony fingers tapping her cheek. "Time's up, stop writing."

My stomach lurches as I glance down at my blank paper.

I watch Madame Mraz's short frame as she walks between the desks, silent as she collects the test papers. I try to collect myself.

"That was super easy," My best friend, Thea, grins from the desk beside me. She flips her shoulder-length blonde hair, stretches out her cramped hands, and leans toward me.

"What did you put for question six? I put—"

"Tests please, ladies," interrupts Madame Mraz, her hand outstretched.

I quickly hand her the paper, and a stab of failure jolts through my spine. Madame Mraz's almond eyes squint at me and I look away.

The rest of the class passes by with more verb conjugation and vocabulary exercises. We listen to tapes of people speaking French, and I pretend to listen. I try not to feel the pit growing in my stomach.

The bell rings. I pack up as fast as I can.

"Rose."

I look up from my backpack. Madame Mraz beckons me over to her desk with a jerk of her sharp chin. A swell of frustration rises in my chest and threatens to turn into a sob.

I turn to Thea, shrug my shoulders, and watch her leave without me.

"Yes?" I mutter as I pace to her desk. My tongue feels like chalk in my dry mouth. All I can look at is my hands as they clasp my flowery backpack.

"Rose, what happened with the test? It's blank. Are you doing the homework I assign?"

My mouth hardens into a line, and I stare at my scuffed teal Nikes.

"I'm trying to, I just don't understand it," I say. She doesn't say anything. I steal a quick glance at her face.

Madame Mraz is a lady of short stature, and we stand eye to eye. She stares at me with a look I've never seen on a teacher before. Madame Mraz's eyes squint at me with a hardness that turns the pit in my stomach into a cavern.

She doesn't believe me.

Keeping my face calm becomes too much. I decide impulsively to tell her the truth.

"Look," I start. "I am trying! My Mum was supposed to tutor me, but that's sidelined because she's in the hospital, okay?" My eyes water again. I look back to my Nikes. My hands squeeze my backpack tighter than before.

"So, I'm trying my best." I whisper, my voice barely audible. More silence. My heart pounds in my ears. When I can see clearly again, I look back at her face. Madame Mraz's angry expression has vanished, replaced by another look I've never seen. Her shoulders relax and her eyebrows scrunch together.

"Is it serious?"

I don't even know. Mum might not even want another teacher to know. Shit. Why did I bring this up?

"Uhm, it's been two months." That doesn't seem to be enough, so I give her the explanation my father gave me.

"My mum, she has, she has a chemical imbalance in her brain. She's okay but the doctors are trying to find a medicine that will fix the imbalance." My face burns. I can't bring myself to meet her eyes.

"Can I leave now?"

She stares at me for a moment longer, and waves her hand. I dash as fast as I can out the classroom.

*Chemical imbalance* became my go-to to explain my mother's absence to anyone who was concerned. The more serious words such as: breakdown, Psychiatric Intensive Care, mental illness, bi-polar and depression were never uttered.

I didn't want my mother to come back and feel like she was treated differently.

I didn't want her to feel the shame attached to those words like I did.

I didn't want this to affect her career.

Most of all, I didn't want to accept that life was different now.

# It's for the Best
*October 13th, 2011*

# Marie

Click-Clack.

Click-Clack.

My black wedges echo down the sterile grey tiled hallways of Centenary Hospital. The smell of sanitizer overwhelms my nose and leaves a bitter taste in my mouth. I stop in front of the psychiatric wing. A yellow arrow points the way to the registration desk.

"Ahem, hi, I was hoping to see someone about talking to a psychiatrist sooner. I'm on a list but..." My voice trails off as I realize I don't know how much to explain. I clear my voice. "I just need to see someone soon."

The young woman at the front desk taps on her keyboard, shifts her eyes from the computer screen, and meets my gaze. She tucks a strand of blonde hair behind her ear.

"What seems to be the problem?"

"Well, my, uh, symptoms have been getting worse."

"Symptoms?"

I don't answer. The lady stares intently at me for a moment and glances back at her screen.

"Sure, I have an opening. I only need your health card, and then you can take a seat." She nods to the full row of chairs.

"Perfect." I dig through my purse and hand over my health card.

"I'll call you in when the doctor is free." She glances at the name on my health card, "Marie."

I shake my head in agreement and walk over to the crowded waiting room. I sidestep over an elderly person's cane and smile at a young mother with a baby. I find an empty seat and plunk myself down for the wait.

⌘

"Marie, Marie Clark?" A crackled voice calls through a speaker mounted on the wall.

I jump up, half-asleep.

"Yep, right here!" I stride over to the front desk.

The blonde lady doesn't take her eyes away from her paperwork. "You're going to see Dr. Tesar," she informs me. "Take this form, your health card and follow that hallway to the end." She shoves the documents across the desk.

"Okay, thanks." I snatch the papers and walk in the direction the receptionist had pointed.

My heels echo down the empty hallway until I reach a metal, white door reads DR. TESAR: PSYCHOLOGIST. I open the door and step inside.

It's a cozy, windowless room with a small desk that reminds me of a principal's office, complete with two chairs, a filing cabinet and a bookshelf. A middle-aged lady with olive skin and a tight bun of black, curly hair sits in one of the chairs. She looks up from her paperwork.

"Marie, yea? Nice to meet you. Please, sit." Her voice is warm, with a melodic Slavic accent.

I glance at her white overcoat and sit myself across from her.

"Dr. Tesar, I presume." I reach out to shake her hand.

"Yes. What is it that you need today, hmm?"

I wait until she meets my eyes.

"I'm hoping you can help me with this." I roll up my sleeve and expose my inner arm. Red welts and cuts criss-cross the pale skin.

"Oh!" For a millisecond, Dr. Tesar's eyes widen in alarm. She blinks and her professionalism takes over. She leans over the desk and examines my arm. She clasps her hands and places her chin on her interwoven fingers. She stares at me, full of thought.

"You did this?" I nod, and shrug my shoulders.

"Marie, I'm going to write you up a form forty-two."

Dr. Tesar spins in her chair to the filing cabinet and ruffles through several folders.

"Uh, okay. What does that do?" I ask.

She finds a form within the folders and whips it onto her desk. "It makes you under the care of the hospital, love, so you don't harm yourself or another." She pulls a pen out of her overcoat pocket and clicks it open.

"Oh that's—that's not necessary. I was just hoping to talk to someone." Dr. Tesar shakes her head and continues scribbling on the paper.

I stand. She finishes the form, and stands with me.

"Come with me, my dear. We'll get you sorted in a room," she says as she places a calm, firm grip on my shoulder.

"No, I can't. I have my kids waiting after school."

"You have a husband?" she asks.

"Y-yes."

"Then we call him."

"No, I don't want to stay." Tears well in my eyes, and my hands tighten around the leather straps of my purse.

She shoots me a sympathetic glance, but her grip remains firm.

"It's for the best, my dear."

# Breakdown?

*October 13th, 2011*

Rose

Rose! Let's join the dance club this year!" Thea links arms with me as we pass the dance hall. We watch girls twirl around the room with colorful ribbons.

Our high school, Pine Ridge Secondary School, is a public arts high school that features a dance hall, two stages, a green room, a dark room, a sewing room, a hair salon, a wood shop and an expensive Mac lab filled with software.

We head to our lockers, shuffling through the flow of students in the halls.

"Sure," I grin at her. "Which one though? There's ballroom, hip-hop, contemporary..." We reach my locker and I fumble with the combination.

"Let's do hip-hop. I know the teacher, he was in my English class. He's in grade thirteen!" I glance over at her and recognize the look on her face. She's plotting something. Grinning, I grab my coat.

"Ready to go?"

"Yep. Just waiting on you, slowpoke." She rolls her eyes. Thea lives across the street from me.

"Okay, okay. Let's go find Elizabeth." We walk out the hallway and push open the school's maroon steel doors. A few meters away, Elizabeth is waiting for us with her iPhone in hand.

"There you guys are. Geez, it takes you ages."

My twin flicks her long, brown hair out of her face. Like me, Elizabeth is short, pale and has our mother's hazel eyes.

"Have you called Mum yet?" I ask.

"No, I was waiting for you. Also, my cell phone's almost dead and I'm texting Ethan. You call her," she huffs.

"Ouu, Ethan," Thea teases. Elizabeth turns pink and shrugs her shoulders.

Ethan and Elizabeth met while they were both walking their dogs, and he had managed to pursuade my sister to exchange numbers with him. That was two weeks ago. Now, every time I see my sister, she's texting him.

"Okay, okay, I'll call her," I sigh. I fumble to pull my Samsung out my pocket. I search the contacts for Mum and hit dial. It goes straight to voicemail.

"Huh. Her cell's dead."

"Try the house number." Elizabeth kicks a rock across the lot.

I dial home. Nobody picks up.

"Well, I guess that means we are walking. Damn. These math textbooks are heavy." Elizabeth grumbles.

"Okay, let's go," I sigh. Elizabeth, Thea, and I lug our backpacks through our neighborhood. After twenty minutes, we arrive at the back gate to our home.

"Don't forget about hip hop tomorrow!" Thea calls.

"I won't!"

We wave goodbye to Thea, and I push open the screen door to our kitchen, toss my heavy backpack on the floor, and pad into the livingroom. I slump into the leather couch. Elizabeth does the same beside me.

"Hey, Moooom we're hooome!" I holler from my spot. No answer.

"She's not home?" I ask Elizabeth.

"Maybe she got called in to work," she responds.

"Maybe." I shrug. We flick on the TV and watch Dave the Barbarian on YTV. We sit there and watch cartoons until the sky goes dark. Around five-thirty, the front door swings open and our thirteen-year-old sister Riley rushes in.

"FINALLY. HOME. THANK YOU LORD!" she yells into the hallway. In a dramatic fashion, she tosses her backpack down the hall, and drops to her knees with an ungraceful thud. She faceplants the floor.

Behind her, our grandmother delicately steps through the doorframe.

"Nan? What are you doing here? Where's mum?" I ask as I leave the living room and seat myself on the hallway's staircase.

"Oh, uhm, your father asked me to pick up Riley from school."

I look at my grandmother. Behind her wire-framed glasses and curly, salt and pepper hair, are a pair of intelligent grey eyes. Today they seem faded.

"But where's mum?"

Nan sighs and unbuttons her wool coat.

"I'll leave that for when your father comes home."

"Wait, is something wrong?" Elizabeth asks, joining us from the living room.

"I wouldn't worry, girls." She scans the three of us, hands on her hips.

"Now, how about dinner?"

"YES. FEED ME," Riley hollers from her faceplanted position on the floor.

We walk into the kitchen. The used breakfast plates still line the table from this morning, and the sink is full with the remnants of yesterday's dinner.

I watch as Nan tries to hide her disapproving look but I know what her arched eyebrow means.

"Okay, looks like dinner might be 'bout an hour, loves. You can go back and watch tv."

We nod and shuffle back to the living room.

⌘

The front door rustles and opens as we finish eating our chicken nuggets and potato smiley faces.

"That'll be your father, I suppose," Nan says, brushing crumbs off her sweater. She stands.

"Girls, can you please put the plates in the dishwasher? I haven't quite figured out how to turn it on." Before waiting for an answer, she leaves to greet my father.

My sisters and I exchange a look of confusion from across the table. I shrug my shoulders.

As we clean, we don't talk or bicker like we usually do. The three of us strain to pick out what Nan and Dad are saying in the hallway. Their voices are deliberately low, and I can't make out anything.

When we put the last dish in the rack, they stop talking and enter the kitchen.

Dad takes off his suit jacket and loosens his tie.

"Hi, loves." My father runs one of his large hands through his thinning dark hair. He smiles at us but his eyes look tired.

"Is Mum okay?" I ask in a small voice.

"Give the man a second, Rose, he only just walked through the door," my nan gently scolds. "There's a plate for you in the microwave, Richard."

Dad doesn't answer either of us right away, instead he turns on the microwave, heating his dinner.

All of us join him at the kitchen table.

After a minute of picking at his food, he sets his fork down, looks at us and clears his throat.

"Girls, your mother is in the hospital for a few days."

A thousand questions and scenarios pop into my head. Did she fall in a playground and break something? Was she in a car accident? Is she sick?

"What happened?" Elizabeth asks with wide eyes. Riley rises up from her seat and hugs Dad. He closes his eyes for a moment.

"Is it serious?" I whimper. Dad clears his throat again, louder this time.

"I honestly don't know, darling. She had some sort of breakdown at a school today."

"A breakdown?"

"Yes, like a stress-induced breakdown. She needs some time alone to recover."

"Mum is stressed out?" I ask in dismay. The thought seemed foreign to me.

"While your Mum's not well, I'll help you lot with getting ready for school and meeting you after class. I'm afraid you're going to need to walk home from school in the mean time," Nan interjects.

"Just for a few days," Dad adds, reading our faces.

My Bracelet
*October 14th 2011*

# Marie

I sit in a green hospital gown, uncomfortable without my regular clothes. As a grown woman, the thin gown feels drafty and my chest feels exposed. I fold my arms and try to ignore the muttering older woman glaring at me from across our joint room. White straps on her arms attach her to her steel bed frame.

I've been aware of mental illness for a long time. I remember when I was twenty-two, I went to see my family doctor for headaches and came out with anti-depressants.

It changed my life. I was so much happier.

Staring at the white ceramic tiles of the floor, I'm reminded that this last year has been a repeat of that experience. Complaining of tiredness, I went and saw our family doctor, Dr. Bayman. She said I was feeling tired because my brain was exhausted from always trying to focus. She made me take an ADHD test, and put me on specific ADHD medications.

They changed my life too.

Once again everything was faster. I had more energy, and everything was processed more clearly.

I was a better teacher. I could keep up with my kids and I felt like the educated person I know I am.

I sigh, wringing my hands. I feel my pulse behind the flesh and I rub my fingertips over the scratches near my wrist. An older cut on my palm has a nice, clean, curve to it. I trace it with a finger.

But the ADHD medicine has its downsides. I stopped eating. The tingling pressure in my stomach I get sometimes is almost debilitating. I get the shakes. Uncontrollable. Unrelenting. Embarrasing.

Worst of all, and I still don't fully understand why, I started hurting myself.

I know this isn't normal.

This one cut looks nice, though, I could make it look nicer with a pattern around my wrist, like a bracelet.

I lie on my assigned bed, arms still crossed. I tried going through the system. I tried seeing a psychologist, but the way the system in Ontario works, it takes a very long time. And the self-harm is only getting worse.

A pang of guilt churns my stomach. I frown, unhappy about allowing the chance for a break,  about leaving my girls and Richard. My mother is around for the next two weeks. They can manage without me.

I need this dealt with.

I look around the room. Nothing but two beds, a table with my untouched breakfast, and the muttering old auntie. She meets my eyes.

"Haram!" She shrieks. "Without Allah you are dead! You're DEAD! I'll KILL YOU!"

I sit straight, alarmed as she struggles against her restraints.

A heavy-set nurse swiftly enters the room.

"Why don't you go for a walk with everyone else, Marie?" She gives me a calm smile.

I shrug my shoulders. I don't want to socialize with anyone here anymore, not if they're anything like my roommate. There's nothing in here I can use for my bracelet though. I wonder if I can find something out there. A staple or a pin from a poster, maybe.

"DEATH TO YOUUUU!" Wails my roommate as the door swings from behind me.

⌘

I enter my room, content with the pushpin I had found in a corner of the hallway. I roll it between my fingers and glance at the bed where my roommate had been.

I hope she was discharged.

I pick up a wet-wipe left from my untouched breakfast tray. After cleaning the sharp end of the pin, I open my palm and find the scar I like. I take a breath, and begin my bracelet.

I don't know how long I sit there. My heartbeat hammers within my chest.

"MARIE! WHAT ARE YOU DOING?!" My nurse bursts through the hospital room's door. With a shatter, she drops my lunch plate to the ground. Mashed potatoes, peas and plain toast splatter across the floor.

Startled, I stop and look at her. The nurse hurtles herself toward a big red button on the wall, panic in her eyes, and smacks it.

The world turns to chaos. An ear-splitting alarm fills my ears.

The panicked nurse rushes at me. I scream and stumble off the bed. She tackles me and grabs my arm. I cry out as a stab of pain races up my wrist.

"No, stop! Please!" I sob.

"Marie! Calm down!" she shouts in my ear. I writhe to escape her grip.

With a violent push from the nurse, I slam onto the floor. My chin smacks the tile and a throb of pain radiates through my face.

I squirm away from my attacker but the floor is slippery with mashed potatoes, squished peas and blood.

Three male nurses rush into the room.

"Sedate her!" screeches my captor.

The three men in scrubs assist with pinning me to the floor. It takes two of them to pull out my right arm. One man pulls out a syringe from his pocket.

Oh god, they're going to drug me.

"No, please, why are you doing this!" I cry into the tiled floor. Tears drip down my face. They hold me tight. I can't move. My first attacker tilts my chin with a firm hand so I can see her. Her mouth twists into a small smile.

"Don't worry Marie, this will help you."

"I don't need your help!" I wail.

"Ow!" The man with the syringe presses the contents of the needle into my vein. My ragged breathing fills the room. They hold me as the syringe's contents fills me with ice.

I feel so cold.

I close my eyes and everything just stops.

# Stronger
*October 23rd 2011*

Rose

"Catch me, Thea!" I shriek. Laughter bubbles up as I spin across the dance room's empty floor, in a horrible attempt at pirouettes.

"Oof... seriously?" Thea laughs as I tumble into her.

"You think you can do better?" I challenge with a grin. We dance around the empty room, waiting for the first lesson of Hip-hop club to begin. As other girls enter the room, we stop, not wanting to look dumb. After the room fills with teenagers, two guys stride into the room. The chatter dies down.

Thea nudges me.

"That's Gio, the instructor," she subtly points with her gaze. I watch the Latino student turn to the crowd of dancers. He wears a fitted plain black T-shirt that contrasts sharply with his shaved, neon-pink hair and ragged, baggy jeans. My attention turns to his friend.

"Beside him is Wayne," Thea mutters to me. "He's in my vocals class."

I glance at Wayne. He has a wide smile and dark skin, with wire-framed glasses like my Nan's. His curly black hair is shaved close to his scalp. He's tall, not big and bulky like Gio. Before I realize my stare, we make eye contact and his smile widens. I quickly look away, my face hot.

"Yo, whas'up everyone?" Gio addresses the group. We all stare back at him.

"I'm Gio, and this is my boy Wayne. So, this routine is pretty much a partnership duo, and uh, to move quicker, I've got ya'll paired up on a sheet here. If you didn't sign up, we can pair you after." The room fills with excited murmurs. I glance at Thea, giving her a half smile.

"Guess we won't be partners then."

"If I get someone catty, I swear I'll quit," she whispers to me. My attention turns back to Gio at the sound of my name.

"Rose, you're with Wayne, here." Gio grins and claps Wanye on the shoulder. My neck and face heat up again. Wayne walks over to Thea and I.

"Hey, Thea," Wayne says.

"Hey," Thea swishes her blonde hair over her shoulder.

"Do you know Rose? She's my bestie." Thea giggles and bumps her hip into mine.

" Ow- Hi," I say lamely. "Uh, Thea says you're in her vocals class?"

Before he can answer, Gio calls out to Thea.

"Thea? Your with Patel over here."

"Oops, gotta go. Bye." Thea skips over to Patel, leaving Wayne and I by ourselves.

Gio scans the partnered groups, hands on hips.

"Okay, Wayne and I will demo the routine, then we'll get started teaching the choreography. Ready?" Gio orders.

"Be right back." Wayne winks at me. I flash him a quick smile.

Gio flicks on the studio's stereo, and Kanye West's *Stronger* blasts through the speakers.

⌘

I stretch my cramped fingers and drop my pencil on my desk. My French homework remains half done. My temples thump and I rub my eyes. I push the homework away, and jump from my chair. I pace my room.

I've been doing this for ages and it still doesn't make sense.

Orange streetlamps light the dark room from my window. On my bedside table, my alarm clock reads 10:23. I stand by the window for a moment, close my eyes and press my forehead against the cool glass.

The quiet moment is shattered by a crash of glass downstairs. Probably the stupid cat. I sigh, close the curtains with a firm jerk, and open my bedroom door.

The house feels empty without Mum. I peer into my parent's room as I pass by. Her side of the bed remains untouched from when she made it a fortnight ago. I make my way by Elizabeth and Riley's dark rooms. I wonder how they can rest so easy.

I wander downstairs and graze my fingers over Mum's handbag that hangs on the coat-rack.

Hearing noises down the hall, I walk further through the hallway and into the kitchen.

I find my father.

He sits hunched over the table, a shattered bottle of Molson Canadian  at his feet. He hasn't noticed. He sobs, his face red and blotchy. I approach him, careful while tip-toeing around the broken glass.

"Dad..." I murmur. I've never seen my father cry before. Scared and unsure, I wrap my arms around his large figure. I pull up a chair beside him.

I say nothing. He puts a large arm around me. The embrace is warm and my breath flutters in my chest.

Slowly, the sobs fade.  We sit there, holding each other among the shattered glass.

"She was moved. You know, into a new ward in the hospital," Dad says, clearing his throat.

"They took her out of Emerg, finally."

I pass him some paper towel and he blows his nose.

"They moved her to her own room. She's in the PICU now. Do you know what that is?" he asks me.

I shake my head no.

"It's the Psychiatric Intensive Care Unit."

# Gio's Basement
*November 2nd, 2011*

## *Rose*

The steps to Gio's basement creak under my weight. I grip the old handrail and with caution, make my way behind him and Wayne.

The dim room is illuminated by one single dangling light bulb. I blink as my eyes adjust to the dimness. Old wooden beams and pink insulation poke through half-plastered walls. I see a fridge and freezer set, a mounted stereo system and a pool table. Open cupboards of shot glasses gleam in various colors and sizes, and posters of beer and scantily clad women mount the walls. Cold from the cement flooring seeps into my pink fuzzy socks.

"So, welcome, Rose. It's cool you can join us." Gio grins at me. Today, Gio sports a neon green tank top with the words LMFAO in bold black print. With his pink hair, he reminds me of a watermelon. Wayne rocks a baggy red shirt and black jeans.

"Yeah, no problem."

"You sure you're okay to stay, though?" Wayne looks at me, concern flashing behind his glasses. He puts a hand on my shoulder.

I think back to earlier after school, to Elizabeth and Thea's disapproving, scandalized faces when I told them where I was going.

"Yeah, why not?" I smile at them, and my stomach squeezes tight. "I'm happy to help choreograph the next segment of the routine." And not having to be at home is a plus. I flash Wayne a reassuring smile. It's sweet he cares.

Not wasting any time for a response, Gio continues.

"Ok, follow me." Gio guides Wayne and I through a colorful beaded entrance behind the staircase that I hadn't noticed.

As I step through the beads, the insulation and wooden beams transform into impressive celling-to-floor mirrors, that line all the walls of the hidden room. Even the cement is covered by old, worn-out rugs. A small window fills the room with bright, natural light.

"Woah," I say to my reflection. I watch as Wayne jumps on a ragged purple leather couch pushed against the right corner of the empty room, and throws a couch cushion at my face.

"You can dump your school stuff over here, Rose."

I throw my coat and my backpack onto the couch.

"Welcome to my dance studio." Gio smirks. He picks a remote off the floor and points it to the stereo in the other room. "Let's get started?"

⌘

"One and two and three and four!" Gio barks at us over his stereo, still blasting Kanye. Panting, Wayne and I fumble through the new dance moves.

"No, no! Wayne! It's step-step-kick-bend then spin! Match Rose!" Gio calls out, annoyed.

"Do it again!"

We run through the moves again, and at the spin, Wayne tumbles into me, and is just able to catch me before I fall.

"Sorry," he says. He flashes me a cheeky grin and removes his hand from my hip.

I roll my eyes at him and a playful smirk tugs at my mouth.

The set ends and Gio switches the stereo off.

"Whew," Wayne gasps. His breath brushes the back of my neck. I step away from our final pose, our arms intertwined as he stands close behind me. I try to calm my pulse, my face flushed.

"At least we made it to the end this time." I puff.

"Yeah, well it still needs some work," Gio muses.

He claps his hands, satisfied with the progress. "But I'm thirsty! Who wants a drink?"

"I do, cuz we did all the work!" Wayne jokes.

"Sure." I pant.

We step back into the cooler first room, and Gio cracks open the fridge. He pulls out a large bottle. The label reads "Bacardi Fireball."

Wayne grabs yellow, green and purple shot glasses from a nearby shelf. Before I can say otherwise, Gio generously pours the Bacardi into each glass.

"Ladies first," Wayne says, extending the purple shot-glass to me. I take it, trying to steady my shaking hands.

"So, uh, what does Fireball taste like?" I stall.

"Do you like cinnamon hearts?" Gio asks.

"Uh, sure," I lie.

"Well, it's like that in drink form."

"Oh, great." I flash another convincing smile.

The boys take the other two glasses.

"Cheers!" Gio grins at me.

"Cheers," I echo. We clink glasses.

My first shot. I think back to last night, the beer and broken glass beside my father. I squeeze my eyes shut, tilt my head, and empty the Fireball into my mouth.

I'm not sure what burns more, my thoat or my heart.

# No Underwire
*November 5th, 2012*

*Rose*

I slam the door to my dad's grey Honda Civic and toss my backpack onto the back seat. Dad starts the engine and we back out of Pine Ridge Secondary School's parking lot.

Dad clears his throat.

"Thanks for volunteering to help me, Rose."

"It's my spare, why not?" I shrug. "We're going to Target, right? What are you thanking me for, its not like I'm paying," I crack.

Dad stares straight ahead for a moment, and glances my way with a half-grin.

"Yeah, well, picking out, ah, underwear for your mother isn't really my forte," he says, scratching the back of his head with one hand.

I giggle at the thought of my father amidst the aisles of ladies' undergarments. He would have no clue.

"Ah, so she said she wanted something that's uhm,

that's comfortable?" He keeps his eyes on the road.

I can't stifle the laugh. "Yeah, well I doubt she wants anything racy, Dad." He rolls his eyes at me, but the smile stays on his lips.

After a few minutes, we pull into Target's parking lot. Dad cuts the engine, and we step out.

I wait for him as he gathers a cart.

"So, your mother made me write a list," he tells me as we enter the store. He fumbles to find the list on his Blackberry. "Ok. She wants three pairs of undies and uhm, a sports bra? But, not one with an underwire. They won't let her have those."

We stop in the women's section.

"Wait, dad, uhh, most bra's need underwire. Especially, uh, the ones that Mum will want."

My dad blinks in surprise.

"Oh, it's not that, Rose." he sighs.

"She can't have underwire for safety reasons."

"Safety reasons?" I ask, confused.

My father runs a hand through his hair and scans the aisles. I don't recognize the look on his face.

"It's a safety hazard in the ward, sweetheart. Do you understand?"

I don't. I nod yes anyways.

"Okay, good. Because, underwire is sharp, and it's the same with anything that could be used as a weapon."

My brows furrow together.

"Why would Mum want a weapon? Are the people in the ward dangerous?"

The lines on my dad's face deepen and he leans on the shopping cart for support.

"No, sweetheart. It's a rule in the PICU for in case she hurts herself with something." My father searches my face. "It's to avoid self-harm, love."

The revelation hit me and I feel dizzy. I put a hand on the shopping cart, too.

"Oh," I say. I think for a minute, letting the cool metal chill my fingers. "So, if she needs three more pairs of underwear," I say, deprate to change the subject, "that means she's staying in the ward for three more days?" I ask, fiddling with the sleeve of a purple shirt on the rack beside us.

"Yes, for observation," he replies. He lets go of the shopping cart.

"Oh," I say. My stomach squeezes again.

"Can I leave you here? I want to smuggle your mother some feel-good-chocolate next time I visit. I'll be in the candy aisle when you're done."

"Okay Dad."

He wheels the cart away. I turn and face the women's section of Target, and grab a red basket from the entrance. I toss three pairs of boxer-short-style panties in my basket. I pass rows of branded bras, trying to find the sports section. Three racks of lacy lingerie later, and

I find them: the elusive sport bras, hidden and mixed in with the maternity gear. I examine the selection with care, not wanting to pick the wrong one. I spot a tasteful black Calvin Klein one, and check the size. Large. Great. I prod the latex material, and check for underwire. Like any good support-system bra, I find it. Crap.

I go back to rummaging through the bras, feeling for underwire in each selection.

"Can I help you, dear?" A plump woman wearing a red Target poncho approaches me.

"Ah, maybe. I'm looking for a large sports bra with no underwire."

"Oh, I don't think you're a large, sweetheart," she tells me with a smile. I read her name tag– Deborah.

I blink, confused. "Oh, no. It's for my mother."

"Oh, a present! How sweet of you!" Deborah guides me to the row of sports bras I'd just looked at, and pulls out the black Calvin Klein.

"What do you think about this one?"

"Oh, I like it, but she wants one with no underwire," I repeat.

The sales lady frowns at me. "Well darling, not many of ours have no underwire for the larger sizes."

"Okay, well how about removable ones?" I ask.

Deborah scratches at a mole by her chin.

"I suppose you could try the maternity section," she offers.

"I guess so..." I say. "I'll give it a look, thanks."

"No problem, sweetie!" Deborah says with a wave. I watch as she turns and sashays to another customer.

I wander over to the maternity section. Breast pumps and easy-feed bras lead me to the 'weaning baby' section. I sift through the underwear, until I find another black one with more padding, no underwire, and in my mother's size. I grab it and head to the candy aisle with my find. I can rip the tag off, so she won't see the maternity label.

When I reach my father, he examines my choices. He finds the maternity bra and raises an eyebrow, flashing me with an 'are-you-serious' look.

My face flushes, "It has no underwire." I mutter.

# PICU
## *November 19th*

## Rose

Riley grips my hand tight. Elizabeth shifts her weight from foot to foot. Dad stands beside us, trying to look cheerful. I clutch a large carry-out bag of McDonald's to my chest.

We stand outside the heavy, locked metal doors of Centenary Hospital's PICU ward. Painted a neutral cream color, etchings of past fingernails scratched on the door reveal the sturdy steel underneath. We stand alone in the silent hallway. Today we see Mum for the first time since her admittance.

A muffled shout from behind the door makes Riley wince. We watch as my father punches a number in a keypad by the doorframe. A muffled voice flows through the intercom:

"Welcome to the PICU. How can I help you?"

"Uhm hello again, it's Richard here with the kids

to see Marie," Dad answers. The intercom clicks and the giant metal doors open with a loud buzzing noise. Behind them stands a dark-skinned nurse in pink scrubs.

"Now, she's lost a lot of weight since you've seen her last, so it might be a bit of a shock. She was really looking forward to your visit. She's missed you three so much," Dad rambles.

The nurse looks at the four of us.

"Marie had a bad night. One guest at a time, please." I glance at my father.

"Rose, you go first, you have the food," Dad urges.

"I need the bag, please." The nurse semi-orders. I hand it over. The nurse snatches it, swivels around and closes the door behind her.

"They have to check all the presents for the patients," Dad explains to us. A moment passes, and we stand together in the silent hall.

Another buzzing noise fills our ears as the steel doors open again.

The nurse in pink scrubs returns, food in hand. She motions for me to follow.

The nurse leads me through a sterile hallway that reeks of sanitizer. This hallway is circular, and as we pass, I look into open doors. They reveal small apartment-style bedrooms lining the outer left wall. On the right side of the hallway is a large circular office, with 360 degree windows facing us in the hall. I note the bars on the windows. It reminds me of a warden's office in a jail. Like an outpost of sanity. As we walk, patients shuffle past in an assortment of scrubs, slippers and bathrobes. They all stare, with vacant expressions, as we pass. I wonder where they shuffle to, or if they just go round and round the unit. Does Mum pace like this? We stop at a closed door.

"Your mother's inside. I'll be in the other room if you need me."

I nod and pause. I grip the handle, and my heart flutters. With a deep breath, I compose myself. I force a smile and push the door open.

Large windows light the small room. White tile paves the floor and cream walls brighten the space. A skeleton that resembles my mother sits propped up in a bed, staring at the sky. Her hair sticks out in odd places, with cowlicks left un-brushed. Restraints hang off both sides of the bed frame. Bandages wrap both of her forearms. As I approach the bed, her face turns. She looks at me with eyes I don't recognize.

"Hi Mum."

Her tired face breaks out into a beaming grin.

"Hello love! I've missed you."

I sit on the single bed and pull my mother into a hug. We sit there and rock together. The McDonald's bag crinkles against our embrace.

My eyes blur. I quickly blink them into focus.

"I brought Mcdonald's," I say, pulling away to show the bag of fast food.

"Excellent! The food here is horrible for vegetarians," she tells me.

"One fish filet and a large fries a la carte," I say, revealing the boxes out of the paper bag. She takes the filet box from my hands and I take a Big Mac box. I watch as she takes a bite and closes her eyes.

"Mmm. Wonderful. You're a sweetheart for bringing this."

"Thank Dad, he paid for it," I joke.

Mom swallows a bite of her sandwich. "How's he doing, love?"

"Dad? Great." I think of the past month. "We're all worried about you, but we're fine. Don't stress about us. Nan's been helping out, too," I add. She gives me a weak smile.

"And school is going okay?"

"School's school. I'm in hip-hop club with Thea." I decide not to mention my new friendship with Wayne, or the fact he had kissed me in the hall last week, or how he makes me feel dizzy just being beside him.

Mom smiles and nibbles on a fry.

I clear my throat. "So, how are you?"

"Better," She says firmly. "The medications they have me on make me very...spacey...very...out of it."

"But you feel better?"

She nods. "I think they'll let me out soon."

"That would be great. But, there's no pressure, Mum."

She looks away. "Hey, do you like my view?" She swings her legs out from under the thin white sheets and steps out onto the floor. She sports blue fuzzy socks.

"I like your socks, Mum."

"You know what, they're the best, honestly. Walmart, I think."

We look out her window. I squint in the bright light.

"I get the whole parking lot. I saw you guys arrive." She points to the Honda Civic. It looks like a grey marble from here.

"Where is the rest of our motley crew? They scared off by the others?" Mum jokes.

"Oh, no! They're uh, outside. I'll go bring them in." I turn to the door.

"Oh, it's okay. I'll come with you."

"Are you sure?"

"Yeah, no problem. Hold on a second, let me grab my robe." I wait as she gingerly walks to her small, ensuite bathroom and grabs her bathrobe from the counter.

"You get your own bathroom?" I ask.

"Yep. Nice digs, right?"

"Not too shabby, I guess."

"I'm moving back to the communal wards down the

hall, tomorrow, apparently," she informs me as she pulls the robe over her shoulders.

"That's good, right?"

"Yep, no more intensive care, just general psych ward." She grabs my hand. "So where's everyone?"

I lead her out into the hallway.

We pass an older gentleman with grey stubble and blue and white striped pajamas. Mum waves at him as we pass.

"My oldest daughter," she says, kissing the top of my head.

"Hi," I say, giving a small wave. He gives my mother a thumbs up, and shuffles away as I spot Dad, Elizabeth and Riley sitting in chairs by the cream steel doors. As we walk closer they stand and join us.

"Nice to see you, dear," Dad says, leaning in and giving Mum a one-armed hug and a kiss on the forehead. He looks around. "So, should we head back to your room?" he asks.

"Well, Rose and I just got here," Mum protests as she squeezes Riley and Elizabeth into a bear hug.

"Ah, well, I brought you some contraband." Dad wiggles his eyebrows, leans in and motions for us to form a huddle. He flashes the inside of his coat at us. Three Cadbury chocolate bars line his coat pockets.

Mum laughs so hard she shakes. "Aw, you absolute angel. Okay, let's go back then."

We all mosey back to Mum's little chamber. Dad stands at the doorway, effectively filling the frame. He tosses Mum the candy bars, and my sisters and I watch from her bed as she enjoys her treat.

"MMMM! I needed these," she says, mid-chew.

"Here, give me the wrappers so we can hide the evidence," Dad says.

"Why can't Mum have chocolate?" Riley asks.

"It's the ward, hunny. Lots of things are off-limits," Dad explains. "like, what if someone has a blood sugar problem, or gets jealous and gets unhappy?"

"Oh. I didn't think of that." Riley says, wide-eyed.

"But I think Mum deserves a treat anyway," Dad says, giving Mum another kiss on the cheek. Mum gives him a tired smile.

A knock on the door alerts us all to the doorway. The nurse in pink scrubs stands with her arms crossed.

"Visiting hours are done now, Marie," the nurse proclaims.

Mum bundles the three of us into another tight squeeze. I squeeze back.

"I'll see you three again soon." She kisses our foreheads."Thanks for bringing them, Richard," Mum says, still holding us.

"No problem, love. I'll be back around nine for the later visiting hours."

"Sure, I'll be here." Mum looks at her bed, then back to my sisters and I. With a brave smile, she lets us go.

# Cold Turkey
## *December 7th, 2011*

## Rose

Okay everyone, starting positions!" Gio barks from in front of the make-shift stage in Pine Ridge Secondary School's gymnasium. Students, dancers, volunteers, instructors and teachers swarm the floors, carrying props, lighting equipment and various costumes. Small groups practice their routines in corners around the space.

"Patel, stand here." Gio points to a taped X on the floor. He yells over the hustle and bustle, "Thea, take two steps backwards." The girls shuffle, trying to match Gio's vision. We stand to attention, dancer soldiers, as Gio places us where he likes.

Wayne nudges me with his shoulder. "Well, this is fun," he whispers in my ear.

"Shh, or he'll put us at the front." I giggle.

"Wayne! Stop drooling on Rose and go back to your

position," Gio shouts, his words echoing around the gymnasium.

People glance in our direction, murmuring amongst themselves. My eyes reach the gym's rafters and I try not to turn into a tomato-face.

# Marie

I sit in Dr. Tesar's office as Richard holds my hand in his lap. We sit, silent, as Dr. Tesar scribbles on several forms.

"Okie-dokie, Marie." Dr. Tesar says cheerily. "You are officially discharged," she says, finishing the last form with a flourish of her pen. "You're good to go home."

"Just-Just like that?" I say.

"You can come back if you feel at risk to yourself." Dr. Tesar replies, "But there are some conditions. I want you to take day-courses held here at the hospital."

"Like a school course?" Richard asks.

"Think of it like school, for people who struggle with mental health issues. It's popular, with a long list of people wanting to join."

"Will that actually help? Doesn't she need medications?"

"Well, medication is part of it, and yes, it's a process to determine which medications will help Marie. But the other part is attitude. Habits need forcing if we're going to break them, yeah? And having an open support group will make you feel less alone, I think."

"How much are these courses?" Richard frowns, lines creasing his forehead.

"Ahh, let me check," Dr. Tesar flips through the pile of documents. "It's twice a week, at $100 a week, for eight weeks."

Richard and I share a look, wincing.

"I'd like to try it." I say. I can feel my cheeks flush as I see my husband's frown. "If they're rubbish, I'll stop going."

Richard rubs a hand through his hair, and looks at Dr. Tesar, perched at her desk.

"Marie's health is the most important priority. Are you sure this is the best fit?"

I give his hand a squeeze.

Dr. Tesar leans back in her chair, and pushes her glasses up her nose.

"I strongly suggest you go to these day courses, Marie."

I watch as Richard's shoulders lower. He flashes me another quick, concerned look and lets go of my hand.

"Ok. So when do they start?"

⌘

I'm late for today's class.

As I enter the space, I hurry to hang up my coat and purse. I had stopped at Walmart to buy razors again. A pang of shame flares in my chest. I move to join the others.

"Okay class, welcome to week three of Centenary's Wellness Day program. How is everyone feeling today?" We sit in a circle, legs crossed, in a large open room.

Seven out of our group of ten showed up today, a good turn out after last week's difficult "Dealing with Depression" workshop.

I think back to how we planned smart goals for ourselves. I had written "eat a healthy breakfast, every day" as my goal. Nothing to do with secret Walmart trips.

I sit beside Dara, a middle-aged mother of two and another bi-polar rapid cycle diagnosis, and Wendel, a sixty-year-old chronic smoker with lung disease. Frank, Linda, Asari, and Reggie sit across from us.

"I'm Deidre, your instructor today." Deidre sits in a wide, cross-legged position called namaste. I can see her black leggings peeking out from under her flowy, long skirt. They look comfy. I should have snagged a pair while at Walmart.

Deidre rests her hands gracefully in her lap, and only moves them to tie her waist-length grey hair into a ponytail. I pull the sleeves of my shirt further down my arms.

"Today, we're going to do laughing yoga," Deidre declares.

Oh god.

I glance at Dara, and see her unimpressed face. Wendel hacks a nervous cough into his elbow. Nobody smiles.

"Okay, everyone into pairs." She claps her hands and stands. We all get to our feet, and awkwardly pair up. Dara and I share a look of understanding and link arms.

"But there's only seven of us," Linda whines. Linda is thin like a ballerina, and I don't know what ails her. She hasn't declared what's wrong with herself to our group yet.

"It's no problem, darling," soothes Deidre. "I'll partner with you and that makes eight. Is everyone all partnered up?"

We share a collective nod.

"Wonderful. Let's get going." Deidre spins with a twirl that ruffles her skirt. She turns on a small CD player and Zen infused chants fill the room. Sounds of waves crashing on an unknown beach permeate in the background.

"Now," Deidre shouts over all the soothing harmonics, "turn to your partner and practice your grins. I want to see the biggest grin you have. Let the music and your facial expressions open your chakra."

We watch as she turns to Linda, gets approximately three inches away from her face, and stretches her mouth into a wide, gaping grin.

The absurdity of it forces a giggle out of Dara.

We turn to each other and try to mock Deidre. We last five seconds before collapsing like preteens into a fit of giggles.

I wipe a tear out of my eye.

"Wonderful energy, Marie," Deidre calls out to me.

"Now everyone, take a deep breath in, and raise your arms like this," Deidre steps back into a wide, open-legged stance and raises her arms slowly above her head. "Keep facing your partner, and on the exhale, laugh together." Her laugh echoes through the room and I swear I see spit on poor Linda's face.

"Say it, don't spray it," I whisper to Dara. She smirks.

We practice the inhale, laugh-exhale for a few minutes, until Dara and I can't breathe or look at each other in the eyes.

"You got a problem, dawg?" Reggie snaps at Frank.

The laughter clears in my throat.

Wide-eyed, Frank, a quiet, obese man in his early forties, backs away from Reggie, his hands up.

At twenty-seven, Reggie sports a lean frame and shaggy dark hair. He shakes his bangs out of his eyes and puts his hands in fists. His baggy T-shirt envelops his frame. He hops back and forth, like a cartoon boxer.

Deidre cuts the music and we all turn to watch.

"Now for laughing yoga to work, we need positive vibes from everyone. What seems to be the issue here?"

"Franko over here keeps laughin at ma' face!" Reggie's hand twitches as he points a fist and a finger at Frank. Color flares in his cheeks. I'm reminded of a kindergarten meltdown. As a teacher, training dictates to quietly go sort out the situation as the class continues the current exercise.

That's not what Deidre does.

"Let's all sit for a moment," Deidre orders, going back into a cross-legged namaste. My knees don't do namaste anymore, so I just sit cross-legged.

"He's not laughing at you, he's laughing with you, man," Wendel wheezes. Frank nods in agreement.

Reggie looks at his dirty sneakers.

"But I swear he think I'm funny or somthin'," he mutters.

"That's kinda the point." Dara rolls her eyes. Deidre flashes her a disapproving look.

"We're all here to support one another, Reggie. Why don't you tell the group why you might be more agitated than usual?"

"But-" Reggie stammers.

"Go on, tell them what you told me at our one-on-one session, you should be proud." Deidre beams.

The air becomes thick and tense.

"Ahh, I went cold turkey on the pot, guys," Reggie announces to us, the same way he'd announce it was his birthday or something.

"Cold turkey? Damn man, that's insane." Frank scoots closer to Reggie.

"Way to go, man."

We all take turns offering our congratulations.

I wonder how long it will last.

"How'd you do it?" Dara asks.

"I got some addiction counselin' from the Ridge Wood Society, just' cross the street," Reggie chirps.

"I feel a little tweaked, but it's cuz the drugs are leavin' my system. Sorry I got a lil' agitated there, Frank." Reggie hops up and pats Frank's back in an apology.

"No worries, buddy."

"They seriously help with kickin' a habit. You wanna stop doin' somethin', try goin' to them. Maybe they can getcha eatin' apples, Franko." Frank makes a face as if he was told to stop eating all together.

I think to the razor blade in my purse. I wish I could have Reggie's progress.

Something clicks in my brain.

I'd never seen it as an addiction before.

"Okay, back to yoga. I feel our vibes returning," Deidre declares, clapping her hands together and breaking the moment.

For the rest of the hour, we laugh. But now it feels forced, my mind on Ridge Wood.

Eventually, Diedre calls us all into a final circle.

"Good class today, everyone. Thank you all for your energy and congratulations again, Reggie." She pauses. "Let's end today's class with five minutes of meditation."

We spread out and lie on our yoga mats.

"Close your eyes, slow your breathing, and still your thoughts," Diedre soothes.

We do as she says.

My mind doesn't go blank. Instead it goes to the blades in my bag, and how Ridge Wood helped Ricky go cold-turkey. The time passes, and after what feels like a second, Deidre claps her hands.

"Well done everyone. Thats all for today. See you next week," Diedre says.

As we pack up, I tap Deidre on the shoulder.

She flips her hair as she turns to me.

"Yes?"

"Diedre," I pause, and clutch my purse to my chest. "Can you give me the contact information for Ridge Wood please?"

I hear the faint clink of the razors sliding around in my bag, as Deidre scribbles down a phone number on one of her buisness cards.

# Behind the Wings
*January 20th 2012*

Rose

We line up behind the left wing of Pine Ridge Secondary School's largest stage and watch the ballet performance before us. We wait for our turn, the last routine before intermission. I watch as grade ten ballerinas twirl in pink tutus to a cheerful melody. I look across the stage-full of dancers and find Wayne on the other side, waiting in the right stage wings. He meets my gaze.

Anticipation fills my lungs and tingles my fingertips.

I glance at the audience and search for my family's faces. The stage lights dim the audience into dark, indistinguishable figures.

"If you can see them, they can see you!" Gio whisper-shouts at me from his positon in the wing beside us. His face is outlined with bright eyeliner and his neon pink hair is styled into a sleek faux-hawk.

Thea grabs my shoulder from her place behind me and pulls me back behind the curtain.

"How's my stage makeup?" she asks. She went for fire-truck red liptick.

"Bright," I reply. "Mine?"

"Perf," she answers. "You ready?"

I open my mouth to answer but Gio cuts me off.

"Places people!" he hisses. The music fades, and the ballerinas rush off the stage. Their tutus brush my arm as they shuffle past.

The stage goes dark.

"Go, go, go!" Gio whisper-cries.

I run to my spot, and hear the rustling of footsteps as the group does the same. Someone coughs in the dark.

The lights turn on and the first bars of Kanye's *Stronger* belt out.

The heat of Wayne's body warms my skin as he stands beside me. He looks to the crowd with confidence. The air is tense with adrenaline.

We begin.

Blood pounds in my ears, louder than the music. I can't stop grinning. We roll through the choreography as if I had known the steps for years. I'm filled with electricity, each step a zap of adrenaline.

Step. Step. Slide. Spin.

Wayne and I face each other. The heat of the stage

lights makes me sweat. Wayne grabs my hand and draws me close. I can smell his deodorant. The stage lights are blinding, yet I can see the whole group as we flow together.

The choreography takes over my mind.

Jump, lean, right arm, left arm. The bass thumps as if it were my heartbeat, and we pulse out the music with our bodies. Wayne's arms interweave with mine and with a lift he propels me forward. As the final chorus plays, we hustle to the finish.

Hop, look, and freeze.

I take in the applause the same way a plant takes in sunlight. The music still echoes through my head. We end, and the intermission begins.

Wayne, Gio and Thea meet me in the wings, panting.

"That was the best." I gush. I can't stop grinning.

"Amazing job, Gio." Thea hi-fives the sweaty dancer.

Wayne comes around and pulls me into a hug. Our skin sticks together with our sweat. The squeeze leaves me more breathless than the rush of the routine. With two hands, I pull Wayne's face into a shy kiss.

Gio snorts.

"Uh, Rose." Thea giggles.

"What?" I say, not looking away from Wayne's dark brown eyes, leaning my forehead against his.

"Your Mum and Dad are like, right there."

My body fills with ice. I spin around and follow Thea's

gaze. My mum, dad, and two sisters stand, waiting for me to join them.

"That's your family?" Wayne asks, and I realize I'm still holding his hand.

I take in my dad's angry glare and my mom's raised eyebrows as they walk towards us. Elizabeth and Riley cackle behind them.

We walk over to my family. Mum clears her throat and folds her arms in front of her chest.

"So, sweetheart, who's your friend here?"

# New Normal

*October 5th, 2013*

*Rose*

So, how's your week been?" Dad asks as I jump into the passenger seat of his big silver Jeep.

I lean into his one-armed side hug, avoiding the steering wheel as his large, freckled arm wraps around me. It feels warm and comforting. I straighten, reach for the seatbelt, and strap in. I throw my overnight bag in the back. The Jeep is new, shiny and spacious. My dad backs out of my first-year residence at the University of Toronto Mississauga's driveway. We head home.

"The week's been good, tiring. I'm sick of Chinese food. Please no more Chinese food. If I see another wonton I'll be sick, I swear."

His laugh booms though the Jeep. Dad wears a light orange polo shirt, belted jeans, and his work loafers.

"Your Chinese roommates are cooking lots of traditional dishes, I suppose? I thought you loved Chinese food. I thought it was a match made in heaven."

"Yeah, well, I drew the line at the pig's foot." Though my dad's brown eyes were focused on the road, I could see his smiling face scrunch at the thought of eating a pig's foot.

"And uh, any news from Waaayne?" He extends Wayne's name in a sing-song tone.

"He's fine." I smile. "It'll be one year on Tuesday," I say, looking out the window.

"Oh, my university-going, boy-dating baby girl," Dad wails playfully.

"They grow so fast." He sniffs.

"What about your week?" I ask, desperate to change the subject.

His smile fades.

"Well, your Mum and I have been to see her therapist. Sometimes Rose, I feel so bad for your mother." I glance at him. The smiles in his eyes are gone, replaced by lines of stress and worry.

"So this therapist, you know, Dr. Tesar, who has been with your mother for a year now? Well, she has decided to stop being a therapist. And you know what? This doctor, she's moving across the country, leaving all her patients behind. So naturally, your mother asked to be assigned to another therapist. But you know what Dr. Tesar did? She told your mother she doesn't need one anymore! And now without her recommendation or help, your Mum must be put on the waiting list all over again. I feel horrible for your mother, I really do."

I stare at my hands, processing this information. I don't want to talk about how hard this will be for Mum. I can tell Dad does by the way his mouth frowns.

"What a lousy therapist," I utter. "Who just leaves their patients like that? If it were me, I'd have a fill-in, some sort of trainee job shadow me or something, so they can take over when I leave. What about all the really needy patients? I mean, Mum isn't even that bad. What about the patients who really need her?"

"Yeah, well, I don't know what Dr. Tesar was thinking." Dad sighs.

I sigh too. We stay quiet for a moment.

"How's work going?"

Another pause.

The smiling eyes are back again.

"Oh Rose, I have to tell you about this woman, my Team Manager. Her name is Doreen right, and she's brilliant, truly brilliant. You remember me telling you? People fly from all over the world to hear her speak. But she's huge. She must weigh over 350 pounds, at least. And she's such a drama queen! Half the team is scared of her!"

"Oh yeah, I remember you mentioned her last week. Has she flipped out on someone else now?"

"No, no, it's better! She's put in a leave of absence for two weeks She's going to be un-reachable. Rumors are starting that she's going to a fat-camp or something."

"A fat camp? Is that actually a thing?

"It is when you weigh as much as she does, hun."

"She's that large?"

"That large," he confirms.

BUH-BUMP. The tires of the Jeep bump over the curb as we pass over the driveway.

"We're here."

# Marie

By the kitchen window, I see Richard and Rose pull into the driveway. I stop chopping the carrots and peppers for our dinner.

With a pause, I look down at the knife in my hands. I repeat one of Ridge Wood's mantras to myself.

*I am in control.*

In my black T-shirt, my forearms remain exposed. I consider grabbing a sweater to hide my almost-healed scars. The front door opens.

"I'm hooome!" Rose hollers from the hallway.

Without another thought, I drop the knife into the sink, stride into the hall, and pull my eldest daughter into a deep hug.

# Acknowledgements

Wrtiting this novel has been like hiking up Mount Everest, and I would have surely perished on some scary cliffside without the support and skills of some very special people.

Thank you Dad, Aimee and Elle.

Thank you Mum, for the open conversations.

Many thanks to my editing support group: Karina Cotran, Jennifer Park Naomi-Nicole Bramer and Anne Servidad. Your skills are so valuble and I wouldn't have made it without you.

A big thank you also goes to my copy editior, Lyndsay Sinko, the person who saw New Normal for its undedited, ugly-self. You helped turn New Normal into something worth publishing.

Thank you Joel, for all the dinners you made, the encouragement you gave, and light-at-the-end-of-the-tunnel conversations you provided. You have no idea how much it helped.

And lastly, thank you Guy Allen and Life Rattle Press, for making New Normal a reality.

# About the Author

Amber Cloves is a recent graduate of the University of Toronto, an avid reader, a cat owner, a twin, a daughter, and finally, an author.

She belives that we are more than what our experiences make of us, and that it is crucial that we all keep taking care of ourselves, especially the non-physical parts.

21678990R00063

Printed in Great Britain
by Amazon